He likes to catch.

He likes to pitch.

Jackson likes his team.

Today is the first game.

Jackson is in the outfield.

He is ready.

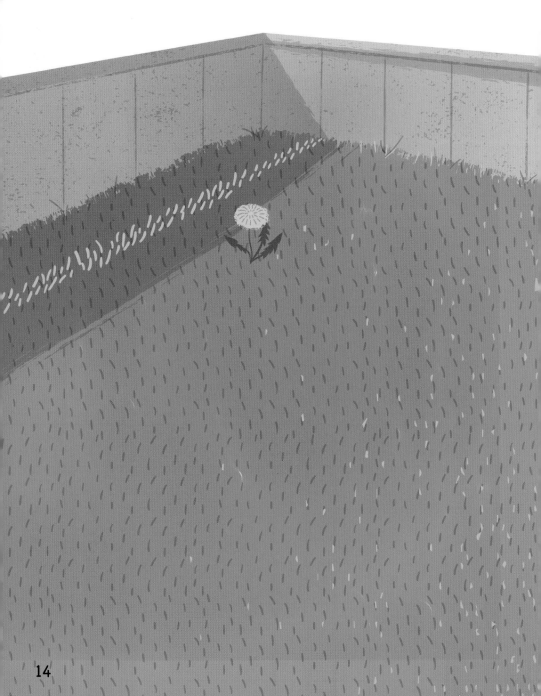

The batter swings.

The batter hits the ball.

Here comes the ball!

Oh, no! Here comes a bee!

Buzz!

Buzz!

Buzz!

Buzz!

Buzz!

Jackson runs.

The game stops.

The teams wait.

The teams have a snack.

The bee is gone.

BASEBALL
WORD LIST

baseball

batter

catch

hit

outfield

pitcher

team

word count: 83

Jackson really likes baseball.

The game starts again.